A
Rookie
reader®

Joshua James Likes
TRUCKS

By
Catherine
Petrie

Illustrated by
Joel Snyder

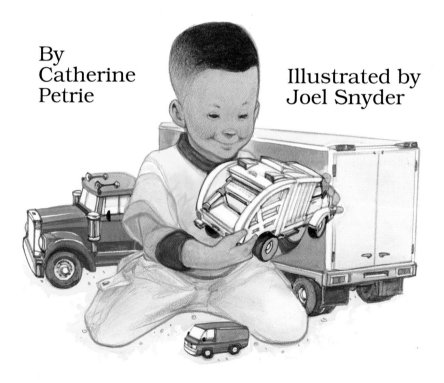

Children's Press®
A Division of Scholastic Inc.
New York • Toronto • London • Auckland • Sydney
Mexico City • New Delhi • Hong Kong
Danbury, Connecticut

Dear Parents/Educators,

Welcome to Rookie Ready to Learn. Each Rookie Reader in this series includes additional age-appropriate Let's Learn Together activity pages that help your young child to be better prepared when starting school.

Joshua James Likes Trucks offers opportunities for you and your child to talk about the important social/emotional skill of personal preferences.

Here are early-learning skills you and your child will encounter in the *Joshua James Likes Trucks* Let's Learn Together pages:

• Compare and classify
• Vocabulary
• Naming numbers

We hope you enjoy sharing this delightful, enhanced reading experience with your early learner.

Library of Congress Cataloging-in-Publication Data

Petrie, Catherine.
  Joshua James likes trucks/written by Catherine Petrie; illustrated by Joel Snyder.
    p. cm. — (Rookie ready to learn)
    Summary: A little boy likes all kinds of trucks, regardless of their size, their color, or what they can do. Includes learning activities, parent tips, and word list.

  ISBN 978-0-531-27177-3 (library binding) — ISBN 978-0-531-26827-8 (pbk.)

  [1. Trucks—Fiction.] I. Snyder, Joel, ill. II. Title.

  PZ7.P44677Jo 2011   [E]—dc22   2011010240

Acknowledgments
© 1999 Joel Snyder, front and back cover illustrations, pages 3–32.

SCHOLASTIC, CHILDREN'S PRESS, ROOKIE READY TO LEARN, and associated logos are trademarks and/or registered trademarks of Scholastic Inc.

10 11 12 13 R 23 22 21
Scholastic Inc., 557 Broadway, New York, NY 10012.

Joshua James likes trucks.

Big trucks,

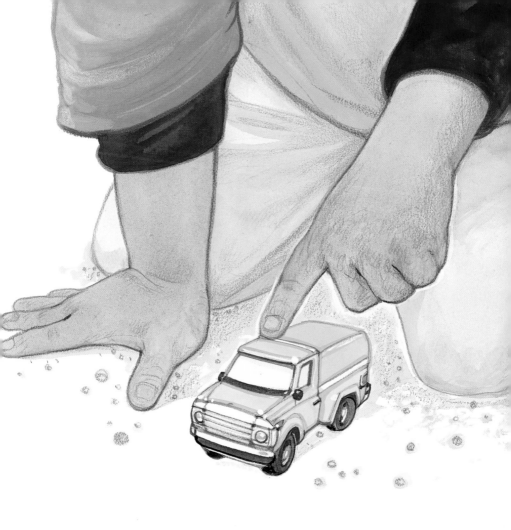

little trucks,

long trucks,

short trucks.

Joshua James just likes trucks!

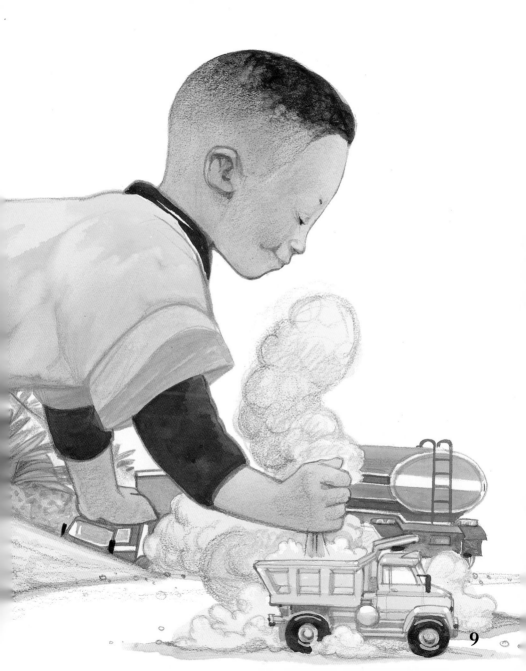

9

Red trucks,

green trucks,

yellow trucks,

blue trucks.

Joshua James just likes trucks.

Trucks that go up.

Trucks that go down.

20

Trucks that go round and round.

Joshua James just likes trucks.

Congratulations!

You just finished reading *Joshua James Likes Trucks* and learned how much fun playing with trucks— of all colors, shapes, and sizes—can be.

About the Author

Catherine Petrie is a reading specialist with a Master of Science degree in Reading. Her creative use of a limited vocabulary based on high-frequency sight words provides the emergent reader with a positive independent reading experience.

About the Illustrator

Joel Snyder lives and works in upstate New York, where he does what he was born to do—fish, illustrate, and give lots of TLC to his son, Adam.

Joshua James Likes
Trucks

Let's learn together!

Trucks Do the Job

(Sing this song to the tune of "Frère Jacques.")

Trucks are rushing,
trucks are rushing.
Fire truck! Fire truck!
Putting out the fire,
putting out the fire.
Good job, truck!
Good job, truck!

Trucks are bringing,
trucks are bringing.
Delivery truck!
Delivery truck!
Bringing all the fish,
bringing all the fish.
Good job, truck!
Good job, truck!

PARENT TIP: Help build your child's language and listening skills by sharing the song and then asking: "Where have you seen fire trucks? What sound do they make?" Explain that delivery trucks bring all kinds of things. Ask: "What other things do you think a delivery truck might bring?" Then ask about other trucks you might see in your community, such as garbage trucks, ambulances, and dump trucks.

Big Trucks, Small Trucks

Joshua James likes all kinds of trucks. He has trucks of different sizes. Help him decide which truck is the *longest* and which truck is the *smallest*.

Point to the picture of the *longest* truck in Row 1. Then point to the picture of the *smallest* truck in Row 2.

Row 1

Row 2

PARENT TIP: Support your child's ability to recognize size relationships, an important early math skill, by enjoying this activity. Then go back to the story and have your child identify the *longest* truck on page 14 and the *smallest* truck on page 15.

Fire Truck Parts

Joshua James plays with his fire truck.

A fire truck has lots of parts. Help Joshua James name the parts.

- Point to each picture of a fire truck part in each box and name it.

- Then find that matching part on the fire truck in the picture.

light

tire

door

number

window

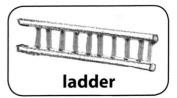
ladder

PARENT TIP: Help your child build vocabulary, and skill in identifying part/whole relationships, by identifying and matching parts of the fire truck. Then go back to the fire truck on page 10 in the story. Have your child identify the ladder and tires on the truck. Have fun naming other parts of the truck with your child.

What Do You Like?

Joshua James likes to play with trucks. What do you like to do? Fill in the missing words out loud to tell about what you like.

I like to play with my _____
                                    name of toy

and my _____.
              name of toy

A game I like to play is _____.
                                      name of sport or board game

I like to play with _____.
                              name of family member or friend

PARENT TIP: This activity helps your child build language skills. After she identifies toys, games, and the people she likes to play with, encourage your child to describe her answers in further detail. For example, you may ask: "What do your toys look like? How do you play the game/sport?" and so on.

Truck-Go-Round

Joshua James wants to ride the toy trucks with his friends. Help him count how many trucks there are to ride. Say this chant with a grown-up and point to each number when you say it.

1 little, **2** little, **3** little toy trucks.
one   two   three

4 little, **5** little, see the little toy trucks.
four   five

5 little children, riding on the toy trucks.
five

All on a merry-go-round.

PARENT TIP: Enjoy this chant with your child to help him build vocabulary, counting, and number recognition skills. Then share the illustration on page 20 of the story. Have your child point to and count the trucks in the circle in front of Joshua James.

Joshua James Likes Trucks
Word List (19 Words)

and	Joshua	short	up
big	just	that	yellow
blue	likes	trucks	
down	little		
go	long		
green	red		
James	round		

PARENT TIPS:

For Older Children or Readers:
Help your child identify the word *red* on the word list. Then see if he can find the word *red* in the story. Talk about the details of the red fire truck. Continue this same activity with the remaining color words from the word list: *blue*, *yellow*, and *green*.

For Younger Children:
Print your child's name on a piece of paper. Identify the letters in her name as you print them. Then point to and identify the two words, *Joshua James*, that name the main character in the story. Go back through the book and have your child identify the different things Joshua James is doing with his trucks throughout the story.